JAILAA WEST

Submit

Savage Security Series: Book 1

First published by Jai-Latte Steamy Romance Books 2020

Copyright © 2020 by Jailaa West

All rights reserved. No part of this publication may be reproduced, stored or transmitted in any form or by any means, electronic, mechanical, photocopying, recording, scanning, or otherwise without written permission from the publisher. It is illegal to copy this book, post it to a website, or distribute it by any other means without permission.

This novel is entirely a work of fiction. The names, characters and incidents portrayed in it are the work of the author's imagination. Any resemblance to actual persons, living or dead, events or localities is entirely coincidental.

First edition

This book was professionally typeset on Reedsy. Find out more at reedsy.com

Contents

Acknowledgement	iv
Chapter 1	1
Chapter 2	5
Chapter 3	9
Chapter 4	14
Chapter 5	22
Chapter 6	26
Chapter 7	31
Chapter 8	36
Chapter 9	42
Continue Reading for a Sneak Peek At Savage Security Book 2:...	49
About the Author	56
Also by Jailaa West	57

Acknowledgement

This book would not have been possible without the support and encouragement of my "Love and Lust Under Lockdown" Sisters. They believed in my talent before I did and welcomed me to write in their wonderful series. A special thank-you to Imani Jay for recommending her great cover artist, and Serena Rytes for, well just about everything, but especially for LISTENING and holding my hand thru this process. Look for the Love and Lust Under Lockdown series and check out those steamy books.

Many Thanks to those who read my first novel and responded with encouragement and wonderful reviews. I can't thank you enough!

Chapter 1

Busted. He stood to face the curly-haired Amazon warrior confronting him from the doorway of her office. His emergency excuse caught in the back of his throat and refused to come out. Aiden had sent a picture with the folio at the break of dawn. When he had twisted his arm into taking this crazy job, but the photo did not do her justice. The jaw that had seemed a little too square and lips a little too full, had combined with eyes spaced a little too wide. The odd image on the 2-d page worked perfectly in 3-d. She stood with her fists perched on her hips glaring with the confidence of an army general. His closed-mouth didn't reveal his awe, and he understood for the first time, the term, "floored".

"You have three seconds to tell me who you are and why you are in my office before I call the police." She spit the words out in a throaty voice, that he needed to hear in his bed. Colt slid the micro storage device into his pants pocket unnoticed and raised his hands to show his keys.

His arched eyebrows refused to completely bow down to her challenge. "I was here today doing temp work. You were at your workshop, and we didn't get a chance to meet. My name's Colton."

"Oh yes, from the agency. Rose did call me about that earlier.

But why are you..." She glanced around still confused by his presence in her office after hours.

The keys tinkled when he shook them again. "Left my keys. Got all the way home and then realized that I left my house key. Luckily Neal remembered me from earlier and felt sorry for me."

She looked around the office again. Colt wasn't worried. He doubted if she'd find even a dust bunny out of place. He'd had years of practice at this and she didn't have a clue what to look for. She walked over to her desk, checked her computer and file cabinets. With everything locked up and in place her shoulders relaxed. The soldier laying down her sword and shield after a long battle. "I'm sorry. I don't know why I'm acting paranoid. You surprised me." The curls on top of her head in a gravity-defying top not, bounced a little when she shook her head. "We're an executive shopping company. It's not like we have any secrets to hide." She reached her hand to offer a handshake. "I'm Alana. Did you say, Colton?"

"Call me Colt." The simple introduction should have been it. Get the information and get out. One and done if she hadn't pulled the one weapon he wasn't expecting and smiled. A genuine smile that outshone the soft recessed lighting of the room and lit up every corner of his dark heart. And for the second time in a few minutes, she had him pinned, face on mat, match over.

He didn't release her hand, wanting to see her struggle a bit like he was. It was a dick move. But when a woman snatches his heart out through his balls he felt entitled. Colt held on to the hand, no pressure but no release. And watched the color rise from her collar to the roots of her rich ebony hair. She slid the tip of her tongue between plump red lips and licked them. Alana nibbled on the bottom edge of one lip. The gesture put him back

CHAPTER 1

on the floor with his cock the last man standing, literally. She dropped his hand and stepped back. Her quick intake of breath telling him that she was also affected.

"Well, it was nice to meet you. I only stopped by for a file I'm working on tonight." She rolled her shoulders and twisted her head in opposite directions, dismissing Colt as she sat down and started massaging the back of her neck.

"Here let me." He brushed her hands and protests away. Using his thumbs to deliver a deep tissue massage to the sensitive sides at the base of her neck. She rewarded him with a soft mew response. He massaged the tension out of her neck and straight down to his cock. Dammit, how could he make it out of this office without looking like a horny teen? Sporting a tent in his pants and a wet spot on his zipper.

Alana couldn't believe she was letting a total stranger massage her neck. She tried a weak protest. But it was hard to muster up much resistance when a tall blond hair blue eyed fantasy put his hands on you and your whole body came to life. His words, "put your head down, close your eyes, and let me take over," vibrated through her body. And damned if she didn't. She'd recently added some bdsm fantasy to her self-pleasuring. His commands were straight from the script in her head. So she did what he said and let the fantasy take over for a minute. Hell after her long day, she needed it. She closed her eyes and for a moment traveled to another space. Alana's eyes shut because her fantasy lover wrapped his tie around them. Her head pushed down not because he was massaging her neck. But because she was being guided by touch towards his leaking dick. She licked her lips and couldn't help the moan that escaped as she retreated further into fantasy. It was wrong to use him like this, but hell he was gorgeous. And when did a curvy girl have a chance to live out a real-life fantasy safely? Her thighs rubbed together discretely. Her head fell forward, just missing the keyboard. His fingers snaked into her hair, massaging her scalp. Then he grabbed her hair firmly in a scene that was a little too close to fantasy. It was like he knew exactly how she wanted to be dommed. Hell who was this temp?

Shit, an employee. The fantasy ended. She was the boss, not the bossed. And she couldn't let her guard down. She shifted in her chair, pressing her wet thighs together and pulling away from his commanding touch. "Uh, thank you very much. The tension is gone now." Alana refused to hide her face and turned around to reestablish control.

One smooth eyebrow arched in disagreement. "You seem tenser than you were before."

"Well, um." She didn't know how to answer that. "Well," Alana repeated. "I have the file and like I said a lot of work to do at home...." She stood and pretended to be the one in control even though she suspected they both knew it wasn't true. His knowing grin burned into her retinas as she fled, locking the door behind them.

Chapter 2

"What are you doing in my office?" Alana repeated the question for the second time in as many days. She gave him her best officer in command of this ship glare. He looked up but didn't move from her seat. Instead, he gestured her to the chair on the opposite side of the desk. Her desk. She shook her head exasperated by his behavior. This was definitely his last day working with her.

"This is my last day." He stole the words out of her mouth and took her bravado with it. "Don't worry, you'll have a new temp on Monday. It was great working for you but..."

"But you're not really a temp are you? Are you one of the owners?"

"No, but I am a cousin. I make apps at home for a living and it gives me a lot of free time. When Aiden called and said he had no one to send, he asked me if I could do this favor and I decided to help him out."

"That was quite a favor."

"Well, it's family and I'm a loyal guy. As you'll see when you get to know me."

"Get to know you. But you said today, was your last day."

"It is, but we will be getting to know each other. I want to take you out tonight?"

Beet red color flooded her face rising like an inferno under her skin. Alana peeked behind him at the door. Almost everyone had gone home but she couldn't help checking for eavesdroppers. Her mind flashed back to the scene from yesterday when he'd gently held her face down. The scene had tormented her night and spurred the arms-length approach she'd used on him all day. "Why?" She blurted out.

"You're smart and successful. A sexy beautiful woman," his eyes drew together in a puzzled frown. "Why wouldn't I want to get to know you?"

"I am smart, which is how I knew you weren't a temp. Successful, also a yes, which is why some men want to take me out. But I recognize the suit you're wearing and it cost more than I pay some of my employees in a week. So I doubt you're after my money." Alana arched an eyebrow mimicking his puzzled frown. "But sexy and beautiful, I'm not. If you had said curvy and nice looking, I would have believed you." She smiled knowing she had him. "So again, why? Why me? What are you after, Colt?"

He glared at her in disbelief. This woman was a checklist of everything a smart man would desire in a woman. The fact that she was challenging him, instead of falling to his feet, reaffirmed his choice. "I don't know who convinced a smart woman, like you, that your looks are curvy and nice. You are old school sexy, a beautiful woman with the body Marilyn wished she had. Some young, dumb, kid might look for an ironing board skinny girl to curl up with. But I'll take my pillow-top over a box frame and go to sleep smiling with you tucked into my arms." He grinned at her open gape. "Oh, and by the way, you'll be going to sleep with a smile on your face also."

"But you don't know anything about me."

"Stubborn I like. Silly I don't." He shook his head in disbelief. "I don't know everything, but we have to start somewhere. That's why we go out, we get to know each other. Your eyes tell me you don't trust me yet. And I'm okay with that. I wasn't completely upfront. I misled you into thinking I was a temp when I am" He drew his pause out, " a bit more. But I know when you get to know me, trust will grow. I am asking for a night, to give us a try."

"Okay." Her voice started off a little weak. But grew stronger as she made her decision. "I would like to get to know you."

"Well, you already know one thing..."

"What's that?"

"I want you as my sub."

Alana's mouth flew open. Rose-colored lips formed a perfect 'o' and he thought again of how tightly his cock would slide between them. "As your what?" She managed to push out.

"Last night," his reference had the color blooming on her face again. Acknowledging that she knew exactly what he was referring to. "Last night was like a fantasy for me." He took a deep breath and shrugged his shoulders. "I don't have a long list of old lovers." She huffed her disbelief but he ignored it. He'd been telling her little half-truths about who he was and why he was there. So he was relieved to share some bone-deep honesty. "I've never felt comfortable enough to explore a different lifestyle. But then you closed your eyes at my command. When I held your neck down all I could think about was exploring this a little further. Maybe closing your eyes with a blindfold, and lightly restraining you." He threw out the imagined possibilities from his long sleepless night. "I would never do anything you didn't want to do and of course we could use a safe word. But the way you responded to my lead was so natural, I knew you were the one I wanted." Her mouth was still open. Had he misread her? "I apologize if I'm off base. If you don't want to explore these things I understand." He lowered his voice and held her eyes in his tight grip. "And I'll still want to take you out. Everything I said earlier is still true. You're sexy and beautiful and I'm not letting you slip away."

"I don't know..."

Alana started to stammer out a refusal but he didn't allow it. "All day long, you're the boss. You bear the weight of that role on your shoulders. I could feel the strain in your muscles and I didn't like it. I don't like the thought of my woman being bothered by anything. So, tonight you'll come over," He slid a piece of paper, with his address and phone number on it, across the desk. "And you'll let me be the boss."

"I'm not sure..."

"I am."Colt stood to his full six-foot two-inch height. "And I'm not asking. Remember for tonight, I'm the boss." He reached into his pocket and pulled out the soft blush-colored velvet collar he bought her during lunch. "And wear this," he dropped it into her lap and started to leave.

"But, she stammered, still a little shell shocked. "But, I didn't agree..."

He shrugged. "If you show up, then you agreed." He leaned down to take her hand and pull her slowly to her feet. Her height made it easy for him to lean in and give her a soft kiss on the cheek. "I'll be expecting you at seven." Every part of his body protested when he released her. But she had his offer and she either would surrender or she wouldn't.

Chapter 3

She fiddled with the belt on her coat and tried to tell herself that she had the courage to ring the bell. Before she could finish asking herself, what the hell was she doing, the door opened. Colt grabbed her hand to stop her retreat. "Uh, hi," She squeaked out. His gaze honed in on the collar around her neck. His sexy smile warmed her chilled skin. Fire blazed from his blue eyes.

He took her hand, kissed it, and murmured, "I'm glad you came." His eyes stayed locked on hers and she couldn't help thinking. She'd be glad when she came. She sighed to release the pressure building up inside and stepped into the house. The slight cleft in his chin deepened when he stalled her.

"Wait," his eyes wouldn't break their steely hold, "give me a safe word."

"Kayak." Of all the words she'd considered, she couldn't believe kayak was the one she blurted out.

His eyes held hers a little longer. The intent stare x-raying her soul, before he nodded his head, and acknowledged her courage. "Kayak, I like it." She almost tripped as she turned around in awe.

"Let me take your coat." He stood behind her, his hands on her shoulders. She took in the art on the walls, the designer furniture, the hardwood floors gleaming in the hallway, under Persian runners. How had she ever thought this guy was a temp? When the security guard buzzed her into the gated community she figured he must be successful. But looking around she felt like a peasant girl visiting the king's castle. She didn't have low self-esteem. But really, what did he see in her? His gasp killed her doubts and she smiled at his reaction to the backless body con dress with the pleated seam. The zippered seam started above the crack of her ass and ended at the thigh-high bottom hem of the dress. He said he liked her curves so she put them on full display. The dress was pure white, virginal in color only. He folded her trench over one arm while the fingers on his other hand drifted down her exposed spine. Fingers going down had goosebumps coming up. Chill bumps brought on by fire instead of ice. He lifted her coils and traced the collar looped around her neck. His fingers tapping the little bells dangling from the collar's end. "Thank you for this." His whisper wafted sensual flames over her nape.

She murmured, "you're welcome." Even though she wasn't quite sure if he was referring to the collar or the submission.

He ran his hand up her spine again, this time his fingers rested on her shoulder blades. His husky voice sent a line of fire shooting to her clit when he asked. "Alana are you wearing a bra?" His hand tracing back and forth, up and down her back, already knew the answer.

"No," she whispered her response, her dry throat making her voice as husky as his. Thank God she didn't have to face him with her answers.

His hands slid down to the curve of her butt, he stepped even closer and asked. "Panties?"

"Thong."

CHAPTER 3

He leaned forward and gave a little punishing nip to her shoulder before stepping back. "Next time, leave those off also."

Alana gasped at his words but didn't demur. He took her with him to the kitchen, stopping to hang up her coat on the way. His hands never left hers as if he needed the physical reassurance as much as she did. Garlic, rosemary, and other spices scented the air, making her mouth water. Men can cook too, she reminded herself, trying to reign in her amazement, as he competently checked each pot and turned the fire off. Soft candlelight beckoned to a table adorned with an elegant flower centerpiece. The elaborate arrangement would have rivaled the most romantic restaurant in the city. "I can't believe you did this on short notice."

He grinned and ran a sheepish hand through his short blonde curls. "And you shouldn't. I had a bit of help." When she glanced around in disbelief he added, "actually a lot of help." He shrugged and pulled her close for a brief side hug before releasing her. "But it was worth it. I wanted everything perfect."

An hour later they sat with their stomachs satiated from the delicious meal. He was a great conversationalist. Witty, interesting, challenging, and sensitive. When was the last time a man held his own in a conversation? They were already finishing each other's sentences. She wanted to take a selfie, and caption it. Best. Date. Ever. She never posted, but Colt made her want to experience new things. "Well," he said, folding his dinner napkin and plating it. "I hope you enjoyed your evening as much as I did."

"Of course." She folded her napkin also. Did she jinx it by calling it the best date? Was it over?

"Before we get to any kind of dessert, we should get a few formalities out of the way."

"Okay," she exhaled forcing her shoulders down. They'd already dined on a sumptuous lemon and pomegranate torte. So she knew exactly the kind of dessert he was referring to. Was he going to Christain Grey her with a contract? Alana put her hands on her lap to twist her fingers back and forth under the cover of the table.

"The first thing you should know is that I have been tested and I'm clean. I always use protection but if we decide to go without you should know that you don't have anything to worry about."

"Oh," She exhaled sharply, "okay." The reality of his words washed over her like a waterfall. He waited pointedly for her to continue. "I'm clean also. I get tested regularly even though haven't been with anybody for a while. As for the other reason for protection, I'm on birth control so you don't have anything to worry about either."

"I'm not worried."

Her eyebrows raised, "Really?"

Colt shrugged. "First, because I'm able to provide for any child I might have and I would never have a problem taking care of you both." He slid his hand to hers under the table. His calm hold stopped their wringing. He brought her fingertips to his lips before continuing. "Second, because I would love to see you grow round with my child. I can't lie, you've got an earth mother vibe, and it's attractive as hell. And with these curves, I would love to see our baby suckling at your breast."

"What?" She pulled her fingers back shocked at his words.

He shrugged his shoulders again at her response. "I'm thirty-three. I'm old enough to know what I want. My dad used to tell me that he knew the first time he saw my mom that she was it for him. I never believed him until I met you. You stepped into that office and called me on my shit for being there. You were standing there grilling me, but all I could think was, finally. Here she is, she's the one."

"I don't, I can't…"

"You can and you do," he corrected. "I know you felt something too. I felt that connection the minute I touched you."

"Chemistry." She stuttered. "I felt chemistry."

"Have you ever felt anything like it before?"

"Never," She whispered honestly.

"And you won't, not for anybody else, ever again." He sat back in his chair, his eyes piercing hers. "And that brings me to the next topic. I'm not seeing anyone else and I don't intend to. You're it for me and I expect the same from you."

"I'm not seeing anyone…"

"That's not exactly what I was asking, but it'll do. I want us to be clear. Once we start this, there's no one else for either one of us."

His blue eyes which had at times been both gentle and patient, now stabbed hers with their intensity. The twinkle from his sense of humor vanished. But his words left her with no doubt, that when he said something, he meant it. He also wasn't afraid to demand what he wanted. A few simple words transformed him from the laid-back date to the boss and she loved it.

Chapter 4

Colt had never acted on his dom fantasies before. She was so freaking sexy, with her eyes looking everywhere but at him. Why hadn't he tried this before, his dick asked as it strained for release. Because no one else was Alana, he answered back. His fantasies had sprung to life in the office when she laid her head down and yielded to him. Letting him be the boss, and surrendering her power. The arch of her neck, the fall of her curls, the sweet moan when he had rubbed her shoulders. She thrilled him when she gave him control. "Come here," he asked, and like the miracle she was, she came. Her face flushed with excitement as she walked. He waited until she made eye contact. She needed to believe him if this was going to work. "This thing is about trust. I need your trust. I need you to know that I would never do anything to hurt you. I appreciate the position you are putting yourself in tonight and I'm not going to betray it." He lifted her chin when her eyes drifted down. "Stay with me, baby. I meant what I said in the office. This is your chance to experience freedom. I want that for you. I want you to lay your responsibilities down and let me be in control of you. My control lets you lose yours."

He asked her for trust and she gave it. He was a liar. He was a hypocrite. He was an asshole. If this relationship had any chance of surviving he was going to have to confess. But dammit not tonight. It couldn't be tonight. He needed this night, to prove that she could trust him with her body and ultimately her heart. This thing between them was true and real. It wasn't going to be easy when she found out. The day of reckoning was coming soon. But he had this night to make her believe in him before it all came crashing down. "You are so beautiful." Her light nutmeg colored skin gleamed next to the pure white of her dress. The black of his collar made the outfit both respectful and disrespectful. Like her it was sexy and innocent, strong and submissive. "I love this collar. Turn around." She turned. Another freaking miracle. "Close your eyes," he directed, his voice gruff with desire. He slid a blindfold around her eyes and secured it behind her head. The blindfold would help to heighten her sensation. But it also hid his weakness from her. He breathed a sigh of relief. Thankful she couldn't see how little control he held. He ran his hands through her hair and bent her head down so that she was in a true submissive position. He whispered in her ear and relished the light shiver his words caused. "From this point on you say nothing. Every word you say will earn you a correction. Nod if you understand."

    She nodded her head in pretty submission. He considered gagging her. But vetoed it. He'd rather have her rosy lips wrap around his cock. He also wanted them available for his kisses. He took her hand and led her to his bedroom. Colt lit the scented candles and waited until the scent reached her nose. A soft smile rewarded him and he melted like the wax. "Can you fathom how bad I wanted to strip you out of this dress, lean you across the table, and take you hard?" He groaned recalling his struggle to control himself throughout the meal. "I was a very good boy, but were you a bad girl." He ran his hands up and down her exposed back. "You came here in your naughty dress. A dress you figured would drive me out of my mind." He gave her a quick swat on her behind to punish her for torturing him. He slid his hand down to the base of her spine and played with the zipper there. Ahh, that zipper. When he took her coat and he saw that damn zipper, he'd barely restrained his fingers. He didn't have to restrain them now. He smiled, rubbing his hands over the globes of her cheeks. Across, back and forth, and then up and down. Her breath hitching with each caress. She was so responsive but he hadn't started yet. He eased the zipper down, opening the dress and caressing the exposed skin. His fingers slid up to the minuscule triangle at the back of her thong. He snapped the elasticized ribbon and enjoyed her quick intake of breath.

Alana's dress pooled on the floor followed by her black thong, and he needed nothing else for a floor covering ever. He laid her on the bed, his hands turning a little rough with his impatience. Slow down, slow down, he scolded himself. He doffed his clothes without the finesse he had used with hers. Thank you blindfold. At least she couldn't witness his fumbling fingers and unsteady hands. Where to start first? Her body laying primed and waiting for him answered the question. "Bring your knees up and spread your thighs apart." He let her lay like that for a minute, her breasts rising and falling rapidly with her anticipation. What he wouldn't give to preserve this moment on film. But not without permission. He needed the trust that he didn't deserve. Damn if he would do anything further to destroy it. So instead he flashed the moment into his brain and vowed to remember it forever. He pulled and rubbed his aching cock, his precum already drooling at the sight. His eager lips could no longer resist and he dived between her thighs. Reading her desire on

CHAPTER 4

his tongue's taste buds like braille. Every bud told the story of her passion. His hands reached up to twist and pull her nipples, while he continued the steady lashing of her slit. A soft moan escaped at his rough play. He smiled. Thank God she was still with him. A lifeless reaction would have slayed him. He lifted his head from his juicy dessert to remind her. "Quiet." His arms grabbed her thighs, spreading them apart. Far enough to be uncomfortable but not painful. No, no real pain. But she should remember who was in control. Her feet rested on the stirrups of his broad shoulders. He nibbled and kissed, licked, and blew on her lips. With every squirm, he held her legs firmer until she arched her back in response. Her back rocketed off the bed into a 'v' position when he nosed her clit. That's it. That's my girl. Get yours. Is this your spot, he wondered. He pressed firmly on her button and hid his chuckle. He'd take her moan and lift-off as a hell yes. Let's see how many more you have. The other two and then three fingers quested into her sopping wet channel. Good girl. Alana had remained silent. So he curved one finger and rewarded her. Hooking her sweet spot until she lost it and detonated. Grinding her vulva into his face and chanting his name. He loved it but uh-oh, she broke the rule. Now he was going to have to correct her.

    He wiped his face across her belly licking his way up her body, taking her nipples one at a time into his mouth. Alternating wicked bites, with soothing puffs of air. His hands kept busy with one nipple, pinching and twisting, while his mouth was busy with the other. Nope, not good enough. Got to have more. Colt's greed took over and he roughly pulled her generous breasts together. Her nipples standing at full attention as he forced them both into his mouth. Yes, his tongue cheered, now that it could lash each one back and forth at its' leisure.

"Uh, uh, uh," He chided at her continued disobedience. Her moans and pleas for more defied him. "I only had one rule, it was an easy rule, right?" He growled between his pulls on her breasts. "And you're breaking it. You broke it about a hundred times when I was down here." His leg thrust harder between hers when he stressed "here". Adding a little bump to the ride she was taking on his leg. "I let you have a taste of pleasure. But instead of thanking me by obeying, you're becoming more disobedient. And I promised you a correction for speaking." He slid up her body. "You need a correction don't you?" He hissed the words into her ear, punctuating his question with a soft bite on her lobe. "Turn over," he ordered. His command rough with fiery need. She flipped over and he repositioned her across his lap. He rubbed each of her cheeks, his hands molding themselves to the delicate, brown curves. Her hands instinctively reached back to defend herself, before snatching back. He caught them before they could completely withdraw. "You're full of naughtiness today, aren't you? Did I need to tell you to keep your hands down?" She shook her head. "Luckily I bought something for naughty little girls who don't know what to do with their hands." She couldn't see the velvet-lined cuffs, he grabbed, because of the blindfold. But her head jerked when they snapped around her wrists. With her wrists cuffed, her hips arched even higher across his lap, seeking his punishment. They didn't have long to wait. The first slap was hard and swift. A little rougher than she probably expected based on his prior play. Colt had been a gentle master, but no more. She couldn't relinquish control if he didn't take it.

Slap! The sound echoed across the room. Followed by the staccato sound of several more, divided across each cheek. His hands stung from issuing the correction so he imagined how

CHAPTER 4

her ass must feel. He paused and leaned down to give a whisper-soft breath across her red cheeks. Blowing each handprint before lightly massaging it. Alana would learn soon enough that pleasure would always follow pain. Her head hung off his lap as she panted in relief.

"Now, you may speak." He softened his words. But not too soft. No weakness. She liked him in control. "Who owns this body?"

"You do." Each word squeezed out between pants.

"Who's in charge here?" He gave her a quick little tap across her gorgeous ass in case she forgot.

"You are." She answered, her voice a little firmer than before.

"Did you like being corrected?"

He gave her a harder tap when she hesitated to answer him. "When I ask, you answer."

"Yes and no." She yelped out before he could tap her again.

He had to chuckle a little at the response. He marveled at her willingness to submit. Thank you baby for trusting me. He couldn't tell her though, no weakness, he reminded himself. "Fair enough."

He hated releasing the cuffs. She looked gorgeous laying there helpless. But her arms should be free to wrap around him for what he wanted next. She winced when he eased her onto his sheets. He again reached to soothe her ache. Damn had he been too rough? He didn't want to hurt her. Not ever. He hoped his rough hands were helping. He kissed her lips and felt them open, deepening the kiss and giving him more than he asked for. And way more than he deserved. Her tongue redeeming him and chasing his doubts away. He didn't deserve her sweetness anymore than her trust. But he was taking it and taking her. Colt's hands took a slow trip down her beautiful body, towards their dusky destination. Her moans convinced him that she was still in the game. When they arrived, they found her cream pooling. Her hips thrusting up, reaching blindly for his fingers. He settled between her legs, and put on a condom, not willing to wait another moment.

He snatched the blindfold off, making her eyes slaves to his. He needed her to acknowledge who was mastering her. But when he locked onto her beautiful raven-colored eyes, he knew he was as bound and helpless as she had been. Leaving him no way to escape other than to plunge in and take over once again. No weakness. His gentle was gone. Demolished in a storm of lust that sucked it right out. He plunged in, back and forth, thighs slapping, his cock thrusting balls deep, and back out again. He couldn't punish her for her grunts, groans, and moans because his were fiercer and louder. They melded together in a chorus of drums banging and cymbals clanging. Their hearts beating double-time as they raced up a mountain and plunged over the cliff.

Falling off the cliff with her was the closest he had come in a long time to dying. His heart pounded hard enough to burst but he couldn't catch a breath. He dropped down, hoping to live long enough to roll off of her. He survived. His breathing wasn't normal. But he had enough strength to raise up on shaking arms and check her for signs of life.

Her shy eyes met his and their lacquered gleam let him know she had also survived. He leaned down and smacked her lips before he gathered his remaining strength and rolled off. Dealing with the condom as he retreated before collapsing back down on the bed. He gathered her exhausted body and tucked it onto his chest. Alana's soft sigh ruffled the hair beneath her cheek as she drifted off. Colt reached down to rub those gorgeous

CHAPTER 4

ass cheeks and did the same.

Chapter 5

The sun peeked through the sheer curtains of Colt's room as if embarrassed by her nakedness. Who was this brazen chick chilling naked in his bed? Not the same girl from three nights ago, that was certain. But after spending long intense nights in his arms Alana couldn't do anything but smile. Colt had moves like heroes in romance novels. Sex Alana'd fantasized about but never experienced. Well never before this weekend. She would never scoff at those over-the-top love scenes again. Colt's sweet kisses had branded every inch of her skin. She loved his soft. But his hard. Oh Lord, his hard. His hard had her on her knees. Literally. Shoving his cock down her throat and showing her exactly how much she could take. Controlling her with his hands on her head, and his fingers gripping her hair. Colt was possessive in a way that made her feel treasured not threatened. He loved her body, frowning each time she dressed. Never satisfied until he found a way to get her naked again. Lovely inventive ways. She smiled at one particularly fun way involving honey. Alana lived in his oversized t-shirts but didn't complain.

    The mind-blowing sex matched his interest in her life and business. He asked questions and listened. God, that was so sexy. He actually listened when she told him about starting

CHAPTER 5

her business. Storms surged in his azure-colored eyes when she described her previous corporate experiences. The insult of shopping for gifts for her supervisors' wives or picking up items from the cleaners. Supervisors who'd treated her like an intern despite her master's degree in business. When she didn't receive the same respect for her qualifications as her male peers she left. He grumbled about her mistreatment and Alana soothed his ire by stroking his chest until he calmed down. She had to remind herself that he was protective as hell. "Don't worry," she told him. She got her revenge by starting her own business. She'd realized the opportunity in those shopping requests. Acted on the demand, and started a personal shopping company. She still shopped for busy businessmen but on her own expensive, very expensive, terms. Colt had laughed and congratulated her on her audaciousness.

They talked about her future business plans. "You better make sure those future plans include me," he warned. When she gave him her "yeah right" look she earned another spanking and an admonishment. "I told you I'm not letting you get away." He growled his words out between the taps on her ass. Then flipped her onto her ass to drive the point home. Rough play was new for both of them, but they loved it. She rubbed her sore bottom and smiled. He may have loved it a little too much last night. But a girl couldn't complain when he followed the correction by kissing the soreness away. Ending the night by making slow gentle love to her. Was he as sad as she was to see their magical weekend come to an end?

"Lana, you coming? Breakfast is ready." She leaped out of the bed. The man was such a liar, she thought to herself. He'd told her he couldn't cook when they ate their first meal. But she found out that Colt had mastered a few dishes, especially breakfast. He fed her his Mama's melt in your mouth pancakes, and she tasted heaven. He only used fresh ingredients to cook from scratch. No short cuts for her man. At first, he refused to let her help. But he later gave in saying he wanted Alana as at home in his kitchen as she was in her own. "You are not a guest," he insisted. "Guests are welcome and then they are welcome to leave." He kissed her on the lips, licking up the taste of his hand-whipped cream. "You will always be welcome." She gave him the "yeah right" look again. This time Colt whipped the dishtowel from his neck and tried to swat her into submission. She dodged him and raced back to the bedroom. Colt tackled her to the bed and tied her palms together with the same towel. Which is how she both lost and won their little game.

"Coming," she yelled back. She moved a little quicker because she already knew how it would end if he found Alana still naked in his bed. She put his robe on and tied it up, when the message notification on her phone buzzed.

"Your favorites are getting cold." She smiled to herself and snuggled a little deeper in the oversized robe. He knew more about her favorites in one weekend than her last man did and they'd dated for over a year.

"Just a sec..." she called while scanning the message. Her finger ran back and forth across the message once more to confirm what she read. On the third pass, her index finger slowed hovering over each word in disbelief. Alana's finger slowed but her mind raced. Someone had hacked her computer system and wiped out all client information.

She dropped back down to the bed when her knees gave out. Her breath hitched and she pulled the robe tighter, wishing for her clothes. How could someone outside of her firewall break through a first-rate security system? Her ex was lousy at relationships but he was damn good at internet safety. She tried for another deep breath, and her eyes filled. Everything deleted.

Whoever did this almost destroyed her business. But why? How? Not from the outside, no way. This had to have happened from the inside. Someone who came into her office and downloaded the virus. Someone who didn't belong. Someone who lied his way inside her office, cause she knew his ass was not a damn temp. Someone who was too good to be true. She wrapped her arms around her stomach, trying to hold back her nausea from the body blow. She fought back tears and did what she always did. She sucked it up, locked away the pain, put her big girl panties on, along with her other clothes, and went to war. She prepared for battle, armed with her bodycon dress as her shield, her ire for armor, and words for her sword. It was on.

Chapter 6

His Amazon warrior was back, armed and ready for battle. Arousing him as much as she did the first time he faced her. What the hell had set her off? Alana was fierce, but she lacked his combat experience. He knew better than to leave the high ground. You didn't go charging down to meet the enemy, you let the enemy come to you. So he waited. "You're a little overdressed for breakfast at my table. You know how I like you...."

"Yeah, I do." She spit out the words like cut glass. "Naïve and stupid. Willing to believe anything that comes out of your mouth and ask no questions."

Alana fired her missile without arming it so he didn't acknowledge the hit. Whatever was wrong she needed to bring it. He pulled off his oven mitts. She wasn't the type of woman to fight him. But his soldier training refused to let him stand completely defenseless. He waited, determined to force her out into the open. Waiting out an enemy who refused to shoot first. The slam of her phone on the marble kitchen island broke the silent standoff.

"Do you want to guess the message I got today?" She fired at him.

"No I don't," he growled. He didn't want to play an effing

guessing game. He gripped his hand into a fist and tried to rein in his rising temper. "So why don't you tell me what the hell is wrong."

"Someone erased every file on my computer. Everything, on every client, is gone." Her eyes pierced his. "But the hacker didn't come from outside, the hack was from the inside. Someone went into my office and downloaded the virus onto my computer."

"Wait. What do you mean every file is gone?" His shock matched hers. What the hell happened? He had put the virus on her computer. But the virus was not designed to destroy everything.

"Are you saying you didn't do this?" She threw the question like a grenade down at his feet.

"I'm saying," Colt hesitated, trying to find an easy way to confess. Damn, he planned to tell her, when she was a little surer of him. But he refused to lie. He owed her the truth if he was going to salvage any kind of a relationship. And he was going to salvage it. "I'm saying..." He repeated again, standing tall and accepting her indignation. "I put the virus on your computer, but it shouldn't have wiped out every..." He broke off when she plopped down onto a barstool. Colt wanted to kick his own ass for hurting her. Her shoulders heaved with a couple of silent shaky deep breaths, but she didn't release any tears. Her distress wrecked his heart, he didn't know what her tears would do.

"Why," she asked when she could lift her head which seemed weighed down by the world. "How could you do that to me?"

"I didn't know you at the time. I didn't know us. I would never have done it..."

Alana's palm shot up, stalling his words, and commanding him for the first time. The boss was back in charge. Damned if he didn't find that sexy as hell. "Just stop. Stop. Stop. Stop." She shook her head, her curls vibrating like angry Medusa snakes. "Is that your argument? You would not have done it to me, but you would do it to some other hardworking businesswoman." She shook her head in disgust. Her lips sneering when she asked the question. "How could you do it to anyone? And then tell me why I was so lucky."

"My name is Colton Savage. Does the name mean anything to you?"

The fire in her brown eyes died down a little and she drew her puzzled brows together. "No, why? And I thought you were Colton Spears?"

"Spears is my mother's maiden name. I use it when I'm working undercover for Savage Security. They are the premier security agency in the city."

"I don't get it why would Savage Security want to ruin me? I've never even heard of them." Her frown deepened. He watched as she tried to piece the puzzle together. "And I thought you were an app developer, helping out a relative."

"That was my cover…"

"You mean your lie?"

"If you want to see it that way."

"I do."

"Okay, fine ." He ground out. "I lied. And I'll explain as much as I can. But let's get one thing straight." He reached across the island and held her hands encased in his when she tried to pull away. "Everything, I said to you from the time you walked in this house on Friday was the truth. Everything that happened between us was the truth. And our feelings for each other, that was true too. You have to believe that…"

"No, I don't. I don't have to believe a damn thing from a

man who lied to me from the very first moment we met." She pulled her hands back and wiped them over her face. The same beautiful face he'd fawned over all weekend. The face he'd admired in every mood from uproarious laughter to the throes of passion. But now he couldn't read her. Disdain or distrust? He winced at either choice. "So, skip the hearts and flowers about us. I'm more concerned about the business right now."

Like he didn't know, she was her business. He sighed and pulled back, giving her space. It was the most generous gift he'd given her all weekend. His heart begged him to pull her back in his arms and keep her there forever. His shoulders slumped at the thought of the uphill battle. It appeared she had the higher ground after all. "I do work from home as an app developer. My cousins own Savage Securities. When I first got out of the army, I worked for them as an I.T. specialist because it's what the government trained me to do. But I also tinker with apps. I love to put them together and then release them on the net and see what happens. One of my games took off and before I knew it, I'm swimming in boatloads of money. I don't usually go in to work for them anymore. But they gave me a start and when they need my help, I'm there for them. We are family. I got their backs and they always have mine."

"But you still haven't told me. Why did they need to get your back against me?"

The use of the dreaded air quotes told him how angry she still was. He hadn't gained much ground, but he hadn't expected to. "Aiden called me in for a job, he didn't have anybody else he could send on short notice. His client's assistant had purchased some items using sensitive information. A silly mistake that put the client in danger. He asked me to retrieve the client's information and wipe it from your database."

"Yeah well, you wiped everything from my database. Years of contacts, purchases, rebates, reward points, tax receipts disappeared. Some of my clients that you erased have been my clients for years."

"And I'm sorry. It wasn't supposed to happen like this. And I'll do whatever I need to do to fix it."

"Who is your client?"

Shit, she went right for the jugular. Damn. He stiffened his spine. He couldn't compromise on this, at least not without the client's permission. "I'm sorry I can't give you that information. Anything else. Any. Thing. Whatever you need to help us move past this. I'll come with you to the office and fix the damage I've caused I promise you. I will put everything back the way it was, minus one small file. My client doesn't need a receipt, or a return and definitely doesn't care about rebates or reward points."

"But you won't tell me who the client is?"

"I can't." He clarified, "Can't is different from won't. Believe me, if I could I would. Trust me."

"I can't and I won't." She shook her head and got off the barstool. She drew up to her warrior height again and looked at him with eyes that glistened with sadness and pity. Pity? For him or for her? "See the two words are different but they feel the same. That's why I can't, and I won't ever trust you again."

Chapter 7

Alana reached up to give Dave a quick kiss on the cheek, squeezing his hands. "Thanks for coming on such short notice I appreciate your help." She told Dave the basic information he needed to start. Their romantic relationship ended years ago, but he remained a loyal friend. Despite being happily married with two children, and one on the way, he never hesitated to come if she called. He understood how important her business was to her and he wanted to assist if he could.

"Who did you say put this virus on here?" He stood up from the chair to stretch his back. He'd been working on the problem for hours, long after everyone else had gone home. It had been a day from hell. She'd been stomping out as many fires as possible, but without access to her records, the brush fire was engulfing her business.

"His name is Colt Savage." She asked curiously, "have you ever heard of him?"

"No," he frowned before his eyes widened in surprise. "You don't mean C.J. Savage, do you? He's related to the guys at Savage Securities. If you mean the C.J. Savage who owns Spears Software, then oh my God! He's a legend. No wonder I'm getting nowhere with this code. It might take me at least a week or more to get you up and running. To restore your lost data…" He shook his head in disappointment. "I don't know." He rounded the corner of Alana's desk where she'd perched watching him. "I promise, I'm not giving up," he murmured and pulled her dejected shoulders into his bear hug. "I said it looked tough, not impossible." His long fingers pulled her chin up from her chest. "I'm going to give it everything I've got. Don't you worry, I'm not going to let it go..."

"What you're going to let go of is my woman." A voice growled from the doorway. She jumped at the sound of his voice. Her pulse pounded. How was he able to excite her after what he did? Anger, she told herself. Her body wanted to argue, but her body had lost its damn mind over the weekend. So there was no way she was letting it back in charge. Alana's livid mind was her best defense.

"What are you doing here?" Why was she always asking him that question?

"I came to help. After you left I went straight to Aiden to find out how the code went so wrong. That's the only reason I didn't stop you from leaving. I needed to fix it." He ran a hand through his hair. Disturbing his usually neat locks. "Turns out, somebody thought they found a bug in my code and tried to get rid of it. Not realizing that the purpose of the bug was to trap anybody who tried to alter my code." His blue eyes singed hers with a heated mix of jealousy, irritation, and desire in one fierce blast. "I was doing everything in my power to help you. Rushed over to install the fix and find you with someone else." He stalked closer to her. "You wanna explain before I jump to the obvious conclusion, kick his ass out and turn you over my knee."

Flames licked up Alana's neck and her already singed face grew even hotter. "I don't need to explain myself to you..."

CHAPTER 7

"You, do." Colt arched an eyebrow that was both wickedly sexy and possessive, as he growled out his words. "You really do."

Dave lifted his hands up, palms out in the universal language of surrender. He offered one strong hand to Colt, "Name's Dave. She called me here to help fix the code. But bruh, that's some code you got going on in there. If you're here to fix it..."

"I am." His firm conviction leading Dave to nod his head in approval. "Then I'll let you start. If it's okay with you..." He turned to her, his eyes brimming with questions.

"It's okay with her." Colt's baritone voice replied.

"You don't answer for me. You lost that chance when you ruined my hard drive."

"Deleting any file besides my client was an accident and I'm here to fix it." He prowled closer and caged her in with his oak tree arms. "And you gave me a lot of rights over you, this weekend. All weekend long, each time you cried my name, or screamed it, or moaned it or...."

"Well, alrighty then." Dave cleared his throat and beat a quick retreat to the door. "Seems like you two have a lot to talk about and I'm sure you don't want me around to hear, as much as I don't want to hear it." He grabbed his jacket from the chair on his way out. "Sorry I couldn't help, but call me if there's still a problem. You know I'm always here for you." He continued calling back on his way to the elevator, making a lie of his words. Damn, was every man going to let her down today?

Colt strode to the door and closed it with an ominous click before he turned around to face Alana. He leaned against the door, his fingers tapping back and forth on his thigh. His face granite. Colt's words squeezed out past a clenched jaw, his lips barely moving. "Let me make this clear. I know that we have problems. But we will work them out between us. You don't go running to another man..."

"I called him for help with my tech problem..." Alana hated herself for sounding defensive. She didn't owe him any explanations. They were over... right?

"You need help with your tech, your business, then..." His voice dropped and along with the plunging temperature in the room. "You. Call. Me." His low voice boomed in the silent room. "Me, I'm your I.T. guy. I'm your fixer when you need something fixed. I'm your handler when you need something handled. I don't ever want to walk in on my woman with another man again. I wanted to destroy him. It was a horrible feeling. And it's not something I would put you through."

"You ruined my business. That's what you put me through with your lies and your viruses."

"And I'm here, to fix my mistake. To make everything right, like I will always try to make everything right. I want to make everything in your life better. Because that's what you are giving me. You are making me a better man. We just met and I already feel the change. It's killing me, you're killing me, when you turn away, walk away from me and push me out. When I asked you to trust me, I anticipated this would come out. Even if you didn't discover it, I intended to confess. Because I want us to be honest with each other. I was hoping that when you found out, you would trust me enough to listen to my explanation. I hoped you would trust me enough to believe that I would never take down a business without a damn good reason."

"I want to hear you out. I want to believe you." She sighed, he looked as wrung out as she felt. His beautiful face, the face she delighted in over the weekend, seemed to have aged in hours. She noticed lines around his eyes and a tightness to his mouth that brought creases there as well. Colt had shown her many faces in the last seventy-two hours. She'd seen everything from his funny to his stern. His eyes appeared sincere and remorseful. Puppy dog eyes, her mother would say. Damn him, she did believe him. Maybe he didn't mean to hurt her. Could she forgive him? And if she did, could she trust him again.

"I'm sorry, I want to believe you. I do. But not right now. Right now I need to focus on my business. I have to fix this problem and you chased away my guy."

"No, I didn't." He huffed, his nostrils flaring and his voice lowering by several degrees. "I'm here. Your guy is here. And nobody is chasing me away. Not even you." He dropped his jacket into an office chair and settled down at her desk. His resolute eyes lifting to hers, "but I agree, we need to take care of this first."

"Wait! I didn't ask you to…"

He arched one eyebrow, giving her the same boss look, Alana had loved all weekend. The look that said, I own you, body, and soul. Her crotch clenched in a twisted Pavlovian response. He winged one eyebrow up again. "Aw baby, I thought you learned this weekend. I'm not a man who asks."

Chapter 8

Colt found the bug Dave had looked all day for in an hour. Alana rolled her eyes. Don't be ungrateful, she scolded herself. If Dave had fixed the problem she would have been ecstatic. But since Colt caused the problem, in the first dang place, she struggled with gratitude. Thank God he restored her computer to its' original state and her files were where they should be. Well except for the one he deleted on purpose. A lot of trouble to protect a client. She wanted to wring his neck and the client's too. They should have asked. She would've been happy to destroy the file. She cared about her client's safety as much as they did. Her foot tapped a drumline on the floor. Be grateful, she reminded herself. But it was damn hard to thank a guy for saving your life when he ruined it in the first place.

He seemed to get it when he rose from the desk and stretched. She slid into her chair the second he vacated it. She went to work, while he paced around the office. She scanned her files. Checking emails, looking for quotes, and reviewing her contacts. Tears flooded her eyes, and she ran a shaky hand over her face. Alana refused to run and hug him. She gripped her thighs, sliding her hands under them as she rocked back and forth with the effort to hold back. She wanted to do a happy dance. An angry dance. A happy angry dance? His eyes snagged hers when she looked up, gauging her reaction. His blue eyes shuttered hiding his emotions. The strain that had lined his face earlier had faded a little as he worked, losing himself in the challenge. A six o'clock shadow spread across his face giving softening his jawline. Sliding his face up the dial from handsome to devastating. Their gazes entangled and locked because dammit she wasn't going to retreat and he didn't advance.

"Well, I guess I should thank you for fixing the system."

He nodded, neither accepting nor rejecting her gratitude. He shrugged. "This problem was easy but the next is not. But I figure as long as we work on it together, we'll be alright."

She responded with a noncommittal nod, that mimicked his. "Well..." Dammit, now he had her repeating herself. "It was a long weekend followed by a stressful day so..." She picked up her things and went to stand by the door. No way was she leaving him alone in her office again.

"Is that how you want to settle this?"

"There's nothing to settle." She sighed. "You had a job to do and it's over."

"The job is over, but not us."

"Colt, how can there be an us? Everything we did was based on your lies?"

He gave her a long hard look. His eyes did the cold flame thing that made her damp panties want to drop. And damn him, as if he knew her body's reaction, he drew an arrogant brow up and gave a half nod shout-out to her pussy. "Do I need to come over there and show you how much of an us there still is?"

"Dammit, Cole that's not enough. You can't control me with sex, no matter how awesome, fantastic, or mind-blowing it is." She shook her head. Did he learn nothing about her this weekend? Was it all about sex? "Is that what you want me to admit? That I had the best time of my life with you, that it has never been so fantastic and probably won't be that great ever again. But that doesn't mean I can accept someone in my life that I straight up don't trust." Alana leveled her steely gaze and bit her next words out sharp and clear. "And. I. Don't. Trust. You."

"I know." He sighed the cold dying out in his eyes, leaving only the flame. "Chemistry wasn't the only thing we had. I felt all the things you did, awesome, fantastic, mind-blowing. But we also connected on another level. When I held you in my arms it was like holding the other half of myself. And baby, that doesn't happen every day. We won't find this with anybody else. We found our home. And my arms will never have a home again if you aren't in them"

His word shredded her heart through the armor she'd tried hard to build. His words described exactly how she felt. She'd found her home too. Was he still playing a game with her? Didn't seem like there was a reason to anymore. There wasn't a reason not to hear him out either. Not after the weekend, they'd had. "Can you tell me why you did this?" She stood at the door, one foot poised to exit. Don't give him a chance her mind railed, but her heart and body overruled it.

He nodded, his smile returning, and she rolled her eyes when her heart went mush. He took her hand and led her to the couch. Setting her things down on the end table. He didn't pull her into his arms but his hands didn't release hers. "I can tell you why, but I'm sorry, I can't tell you who." Her back stiffened ramrod straight. What was the freaking point if he was only going to give her more half-truths? He was wasting her time, she fumed. Her anger fired up like a big rig at a monster truck rally. He let her pull her hand away, but only so that his hands could frame

CHAPTER 8

her face. "Let me tell you why. And then you decide if you still need to know who."

"And if I still need to know who?"

"Then baby, I promise, I will call and ask the client's permission. That's non-negotiable. I would never sell you out to somebody else. No matter what they offered. I will always give you my loyalty. Because I care about you, and because you're mine." His eyes caressed hers, his rough palms gentle on her face. "But also because I'm a loyal guy. I took this case out of loyalty. I would never ask you to be less than who you are. And I can't be less than who I am either."

She nodded her head. He almost ruined her business. But she was growing aroused as hell at his fierce loyalty. How long had she wished for a man who understood the definition of the word? A man who was willing to give it unconditionally? "Okay," she acquiesced. "I'm listening."

His explanation didn't take long. Their client was very famous. But she paid for her fame with an intelligent, persistent, and dangerous stalker. A stalker who managed to find her no matter how many addresses, phones, homes, or aliases she used. He'd broken into her home and attacked her twice. She was lucky that she'd been saved each time. But she was afraid that her luck was running out. When her last assistant purchased some items on her behalf, he messed up. He used her real name and current address, putting her in extreme danger once again. Colt sighed. "Aiden called me to get her information stripped from the computer. I would have taken the information and been in and out if you hadn't arrived and nunchuked me."

"I did not use any nunchucks on you." She laughed at his words.

"Babe, you definitely nunchucked me. Put the smackdown,

laid me out, however you want to put it." He shook his head, do you think I've ever messed up on a code before? I always run a scan to make sure the program is running properly. I saw you and I was flummoxed. And that is not a word I have ever used before. You were it."

Her face flushed with pleasure at his flattery even as she denied it, with a shake of her head. "Anyway... Continue with the story. Don't try to change the subject."

He shrugged. "End of story. My job here was about protecting a friend. Not hurting anyone. Savage Security is about protecting others. We stand for people in trouble."

"Why didn't Savage Security reach out to me? If you had explained the situation, I would have worked with you. Helped your client out, after all, she's my client too."

"We couldn't take the chance. We didn't know you. You might have been a reputable person and helped. But what if you decided to keep her information and sell it later? We were on a tight schedule. There was no time to investigate you to see if you were one of the good guys. And even if you were. What about the other employees? How many people could access the information? He threw his hands up. "Too many people to investigate and not enough time to do it."

"And you still can't tell me her name?"

He shook his head, his shoulders drooping. "Not without her permission. I'm sorry." He ran a weary hand through his cropped curls and she wanted to brush his hand aside and take over. She remembered how those soft curls had brushed the insides of her thighs. Her hands running through them to rake his scalp when she led him to the crevice between her legs. "We got lucky," he continued, unaware of wandering thoughts. "She caught the mistake before the order went out. We think we stopped it in time, but this guy is scary good. Even I can't figure out how he is able to find her online."

Alana shook her head, her brows furrowing. How would she feel if she were in her client's shoes? Would she do everything in her power to stop him? Hell yeah, without any doubt. She would whatever she could to fight. But how do you fight a ghost? She shook her head again. Thank God she had men like Colt and the Savage team on her side. No matter how rich or famous you were, it must be terrifying to have someone obsessed with you. "I hope you guys stopped any damage before it happened. I hate thinking he might be able to reach her because of my company."

"We don't think he will. But we are getting her the best protection around to cover her twenty-four seven. Beau will be her shadow until we catch this guy. He's an ex-navy seal. Scary protective, the best at his job. If this guy breaks into her home again, it will be the last time." His eyes snagged hers again. "Now you've heard the whole story. My question for you is…are we good?"

Chapter 9

"Are we good?" The question haunted her as she followed Colt back to his place. She'd answered yes and meant it. She admired him for his loyalty to his client. She felt the same loyalty to hers. Would she go as far as he did? Nope, no way. She loved her clients but not enough to break the law for them. Colt broke the law and didn't apologize for it. He decided it needed to be done and he did it. An extreme solution to an extreme problem. Could she accept that? During the weekend he had asked for her trust, over and over. She'd fooled herself into thinking he meant sexually. But now she knew better. Now she understood he meant every way and every day. He jumped into the pool, diving straight into the deep end with his feelings. His reckless deep-dive scared her. She preferred to drag her foot along the edge of the pool before proceeding with caution down the stairs. Slowly making her way to the deep end of feelings. Opposites, she grimaced to herself. Could opposites work in a relationship? Did she want it to work? He wasn't going to be easy. He wasn't going to be a guy she could slide into and out of a relationship.

Alana jumped, her heart thundering in her chest when he knocked on her car window. "You ready?" He asked her about exiting the car. She met his eyes through the glass. Was she

CHAPTER 9

ready for a relationship with him?

"Sure," she opened her door and took his hand. Alana saw his eyes smoldering when they locked on her face. Yes, she was sure of their chemistry. But unsure if it was enough. The heat rising from her sex and spreading through her body whispered yes. Yes, absolutely, because no one had evoked this passion before.

He pulled her inside the house and secured her in his arms. His hands strong, firm and caring at the same time. She ran her hands up and down his back, soothing his rapid breathing. What the hell? His heart raced as if he had run a marathon uphill. "Hey," she pulled back and ran her hand down the side of his jaw, concerned by the emotions racing across his face. "Are you okay?"

"Yeah." He steadied himself by looking into her eyes. "Yeah, I am now." His lips caressed hers with each word. His warm breath fanning across her face. "I almost lost you." His forehead rested on hers, his gaze tied to their entwined fingers. "And I was not okay. That was not okay at all. Don't get me wrong, I was not," He growled the word at her and repeated it. "Not going to let you go. But it was still scary as hell. It's one helluva scary roller coaster to be on, meeting you and then almost losing you. My head is spinning now that the roller coaster is back on level ground."

"I agree." She kissed his lips. "Same roller coaster, same head spin. But we're here now and that's got to count for something."

Air wooshed from her lungs as he swept her into his arms, carrying her towards his bedroom. "It counts for a lot. It counts for everything." He leaned down to kiss her before splaying her on his bed. He stood up and started stripping. His eyes never left her. His eyes lingered on every inch of skin she exposed. Silence.

Not uncomfortable, not eerie. Just silent. Like church. Like worship. He took his time and so she waited for him to speak. When he spoke, it was with hands and lips, fingers and touches. Gestures and caresses communicating more than words and ending in a flurry of grunts and moans. He pulled her up another roller coaster ascent. Her heart pounded as she raced up the high peaks, levitating in midair. Then floating in a free fall before he plummeted her back to earth only to sweep her up to another high peak. God, she was flying, heart-pounding, body shaking, on the roller coaster. She gave a corkscrew swirl and clamped her muscles down on his shaft. Pumping him to the drumbeat coursing through her veins. She wanted to give him the same head spin. Hell no, she wasn't in this alone. She battered him, until both hearts pounded together. And they lay exhausted on top of each other. His cock pulsing like mad inside of her keeping time with the erratic beat of their hearts. She found her certain when he collapsed onto her, pulling out at the same time. Don't go, she whispered in reflex. And like the stars still bursting behind her closed lids, she realized her truth. She never wanted him to leave. The connection they had was undeniable. She summoned the energy to wipe the sweat pooling on his back. Her hand swiped down to the curve of his butt cheeks. Enjoying the feel of his skin morphing into hers. Her legs remained crossed over his thighs in a hard embrace. An embrace she wasn't in any hurry to release.

Once again, she was alone in Cole's wrecked bed, when a

CHAPTER 9

message notification woke her. Colt's phone pealed for the third time so she reached over to silence it. She couldn't miss the onscreen messages. I missed you last night. Why didn't you stop by? You know you can come over any time. She'd believed him when he said they were exclusive. But the provocative messages slashed her heartstrings making them drop. Who was "Elle"? And if he had carte blanch to drop in on her at any time then why was he wasting time with her? She didn't want to jump to any conclusions. She hated feeling insecure. Last night he had pounded his devotion into her body, every stroke wiping away doubts. But she couldn't help asking anyway. Was she a fool?

"Aww Baby, I wanted you to sleep in. I was gonna surprise you with breakfast in bed." His words rumbled over his shoulder as he finished the last touches of a breakfast tray. "Go back in the bed, I wasn't finished with you yet. Making you a little sustenance to help you keep your strength up for our next go-round." The light from his sunny grin extinguished when he turned around and saw her stoic face. "What's wrong?" His deep voice rumbled across the room.

"Elle texted you. She wondered why you didn't stop by last night. And to tell you she misses you..."

"Misses me?" His brow furrowed. "Oh, she missed my call, is probably what she meant. I called her yesterday. We played phone tag." He set the tray down on the island and assessed the grave look on her face.

"Yeah, well, she says you could have just dropped by. Apparently, you guys have that type of relationship."

His blue eyes hardened as they watched her in stony silence, his jaw ticking in agitation. "You let me have access to your business files and computers, even though you knew I was responsible for the virus. Then we came here and you gave me every part of your body. Every. Part. I had you in every way. But this morning, because of a goddamn text, you don't trust me?" His voice rose cracking like ice dropping into a glass.

"Don't ask me about trust. I'm asking you about a woman calling you and inviting you over."

"No, you didn't ask me a thing? You just threw the message out there and expect me to defend myself against whatever you are imagining."

"Fair enough. I won't have to imagine anything if you just tell me who she is and what is she to you?"

He ran an aggrieved hand over his face, his flaring nostrils taking in a deep breath. "First tell me. Do you trust me? Not just with your body, but with your heart? Do you believe I would ever do anything to hurt you, again? Do you think I would beg you?" His voice rasped his questions with a sub-zero intensity. "I begged you to give me your trust. Do you think I would do that if I wasn't worthy of it? Do you think I'm that guy?" His eyes held hers, no blinking, no wavering, and no release.

Flashes of the past few days spun through her mind. He had been a caring concerned partner every step of the way. Bossy, domineering, possessive, infuriating but in the end, she'd given him her trust and more and she didn't regret it. When she told him she accepted his reasons for his actions she meant it. Now he was asking for something more. Pushing for more. Could she give it? "I trust you Colt." He leaned forward and braced his arms on the countertop. He exhaled and dropped his head down. His shoulders shuddered with his ragged breathing before he stood up to his full height and met her eyes again. Colt came around the island, reaching for her. But she stepped back, evading his hands and throwing up a palm to stop his march. "I guess, I don't need to know who Elle is. Instead, I need to know who I am?" His brow furrowed and he squinted his eyes. "Who am I to you?" Her vision blurred and she bit her lip. Another roller coaster, another breathless ride paused at the top. She looked at the worry lines creasing his face. She couldn't comfort him, or whatever he needed from her. She looked around the kitchen and wondered, how had they gotten here? How had he wormed his way into her heart so fast? But there he was, so deep that if he moved it would rip apart. Was she in his heart as well? If not, wrenching that hook out of her heart was gonna hurt sooo bad.

He pushed her palm out of the way and pulled her into his arms, halting her retreat. "Who are you to me?" He shook her shoulders before crushing her to himself. "You are my air. My breath. My heart. You are my world, my everything. I love you. You were the reason I got out of bed this morning, and the reason I can't wait to return to it. I don't know how I got so goddamn lucky to find you but you are the one I never want to lose. You are the one I want to be with, every day, for the rest of our lives. I want to build a family with you, a home with you, a...."

"Okay, okay," she laughed sniffed. Her tears burst through their dam. Pushed up and out by the fullness of her heart. "Don't make me go all Jerry Maguire on you. You had me at... well... Ok, at whatever you said first. Damn it. You had me at whatever the hell you said first." She raised her hand and held the sides of his face. Her beautiful brown eyes merging into his blue ones. "And I love you too." She kissed him long and hard. Until she couldn't tell where his tongue ended and her tongue began. Until she couldn't tell whose hands were holding tighter, longer. Until her chest and his welded together. Until his breath and hers, their heartbeats became one.

Alana told him later that people were going to think they were crazy. He told her that he couldn't care less. He told her that Elle was his mysterious client and he'd been trying like crazy to reach her and get her permission to share her information. And she told him she couldn't care less. Because in the end, all that really mattered was how they felt about each other.

Continue Reading for a Sneak Peek At Savage Security Book 2: Obey

Elle sauntered her voluptuous ass to the door and let Beau in four minutes after he rang the bell. In one more minute, he would have been out of there. And Aiden could kiss his ass. Somethings were not worth the trouble. Especially spoiled starlets who made him wait after her security buzzed him into the ultra-private gated community. If they were going to work together then he needed to establish some ground rules. And he didn't give two flips about how damn beautiful or sexy she was.

"I'm sorry to keep you waiting. I was on an important phone call and I..."

"And you couldn't be bothered to respect my time." His tolerance for bull was at an all-time low since his return to civilian life. And he didn't tolerate games or disrespect from anyone.

Her eyes blazed defiance before banking down to cool embers. She didn't offer any more excuses and he was glad 'cause he didn't want to hear any. "As I said, I apologize." Her tepid voice didn't freeze him out or try to warm him up. It reminded him of the bland brackish water he'd had to drink during missions in Iraq. Water that gave hydration without relieving burning thirst.

She invited him in and closed the door. "You are Mr. Rockland, from Savage Security, correct?"

"Shouldn't you have found that out and checked my identification, before you let me in the house and closed the door?" He growled, angry at her carelessness.

Her hand went to her neck, with a small tremor, that was quickly quelled when she lowered her hand back to her side. "Yes, you're right of course. I was on the phone with Aiden, who told me to expect you, and I assumed they checked your id at the gate?"

"They did check my id." He rolled over her response. "But they are not responsible for your safety. You are. Your safety depends on you and your choices. You have to take that responsibility. I'm here to help protect you until we catch this frigging asshole. But I can't help you more than you can help yourself." His voice lowered and he paused to judge her reaction. Either she'd heed his advice and he'd stay or she wouldn't and he was out. "So from now on, you check every person, every id. Unless I clear somebody. You check and double-check."

She raised a manicured brow and nodded her head in submission before she challenged him. "In that case, may I see some identification?"

So she did have a little spark, good, a little spark might save her life. "Right here." He whipped out his identification and approved when she took her time to read each line. "Remember nobody should mind doing this. Nobody should be excluded from doing this. Only people you are familiar with. And I like how you're checking each fact. Most people just glance at the picture, even fewer people check the name. And almost no one reads the details. But the details are harder to fake." Her steady gaze never wavered as she returned the card. "If I steal the id from the cable guy and put my picture on his id. I can give you his name. But if his id says he weighs one-twenty and I clearly weigh three hundred pounds. That's much harder to fake. So always check everything."

"Okay." She nodded. "Your id doesn't mention Savage Security, it says Hexagon?"

"Good job." Thank God, she wasn't a complete idiot and applied his advice. "Yeah, I don't actually work for Aiden at Savage. They specialize in corporate espionage, internet security, the spy stuff. I worked with them for a while but I needed more active assignments and decided to go a different way. I started a protection service with some of my ex-seals, who needed to be more than desk jockeys. Now I partner with Aiden when he needs muscle and he partners with me when I need..."

"Brains," she interjected.

He raised a brow at that. "Tech." Spark was okay. Sarcasm, not so much. "I'm plenty smart baby girl. But I prefer to let my actions speak louder than my words." He started walking through the house. He gave each room a brief once over, before settling on a stool in the kitchen. "Now why don't you tell me why you need a bodyguard, with Navy Seal experience?"

"Aiden didn't tell you anything?"

"He told me you had a stalker. Not so unusual in your case. A beautiful girl with a high social media profile." He shrugged. "Not surprising. But he insisted that I specifically take the case. That's like sending an army after a shoplifter. Something is worrying him more than your usual stalker case. So why don't you tell me what it is."

"My name is Ella Azarola."

"I thought it was…"

"Lexy?" She frowned, her brows furrowing in agitation. Dammit, she should never have that pained look. He wanted to kiss that frown away. Sweep kisses across her forehead until her expression was all pleasure, no pain. Only five minutes with her and she was already sucking him under her spell.

He swallowed hard and focused. But he couldn't stop his voice from coming out rough as gravel. "Can't blame me for that. Everybody knows Sexy Lexy. Especially when you're all over the media. You've been internet famous and then reality tv famous ever since that video…"

Fire flamed to life in her coal-black irises, at the mention of the video. She didn't like it, but she couldn't deny its' existence. He doubted there was any adult who didn't know about her

Sexy Lexy tape. "Yeah well, that video is six years old now. And the guy on the tape was calling me by a stupid nickname he made up from Alexis, my middle name." She stopped mid-sentence and took her hair down only to twist it back up into the same top knot. Her shoulders rose and fell while she visibly extinguished the fire before continuing. "Anyway because I had crossed the eighteen line two weeks earlier, it was okay to release, sell and distribute it without my permission and not get arrested for child pornography. And no matter how I tried to fight it, and I tried hard at first, it was impossible. The more I fought it, the more famous I became, and the tape spread faster than a virus in a nursery school. Until eventually everyone everywhere knew about Sexy Lexy. Stalkers and psychos come at me routinely." She shook her head, her shoulders weighed down by boulders. "I've needed armed security since I was eighteen years old. Believe me, I know the drill. But this guy is different."

"How so?"

"First he takes his psychosis to the next level. I've had some who were jealous of the guy in the video, others who hated the guy in the video. But this guy insists he is the guy in the video."

"Could he be?"

"No, first of all, we still run in the same circle. Unfortunately. He even tried to date my best friend." A quick eye-roll accompanied her words.

"Jealous?"

"Not. At. All." Her jaw hardened and lent a firm cadence to her words. She continued as if she were reporting on a cold case file. "This guy is different not only because of his claim but because he is a genius at tech. He has located me from one end of this country to the next. He is one of the few who knows my actual name. I usually use, Sexy Lexy or Lexy and I reserve Ella for close friends. Most of whom call me Elle. It's close to my real name and it helps with anonymity. But when I use my real name, he's able to track me. And when I say track, I mean every activity, address, hotel, and phone. And he gets close. He has been inside three of my previous homes. He finds me even if my social media says I'm somewhere else. A couple of days ago I had an assistant buy something for me. He was supposed to use one of my aliases. But he forgot and gave my real name to the company. And even though Savage had someone wipe my information from their computer it was too late. I started getting harassing phone calls immediately."

"Did you work with the police on this?"

"I tried but they aren't real helpful. They're either requesting autographs or staring at me like I'm a diseased cat pooping on their paperwork. I think they are okay with finding the guy after something happens to me. I know most of them think this is an elaborate publicity stunt."

"And is it?"

Look for Savage Security Book 2: February 2021

About the Author

Jailaa West grew up on the southside of Chicago. She fell hard for romance books in junior high school when she got her first book boyfriend. Aww, she remembers it like it was yesterday. That first kiss. When he swore his undying love. When they married in the epilogue. When it ended. Say what now? She quickly found another book boyfriend and then another and yet another. She's been book-in-love quite a few times now and she loves it as much as the first time.

For more information, updates, ARC opportunities and giveaways be sure to follow Jailaa...

You can connect with me on:
- https://www.jailaawest.com
- https://www.facebook.com/groups/jailaawestbooks

Subscribe to my newsletter:
- http://eepurl.com/hmBvhn

Also by Jailaa West

Thanksgiving with the Naughty Boss
Love and Lust Under Lockdown Book 2

Troy trusts no one, after his former lover betrayed him and almost destroyed his business. Now he's forced to quarantine with Ava and work on rebuilding what was lost. He must open his home to her, but can he also open his heart? This short steamy romance will melt your heart. Free with Kindle Unlimited. $0.99 without https://www.amazon.com/Thanksgiving-Naughty-Boss-Under-Lockdown-ebook/dp/B08NSJXMQ9/ref=cm_cr_arp_d_product_top?ie=UTF8

Printed in Great Britain
by Amazon